Little Katie Goes to the Moon

Written and Illustrated by

Carmela Dutra

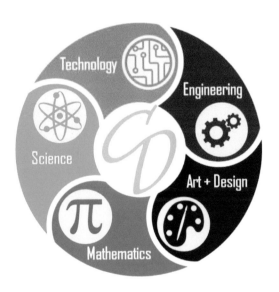

Nothing is more important than creative play through imagination.
Never stop playing, and never stop imagining!

Carmela Dutra

First Edition: April 2016

Published in North America by Carmela Dutra. For information, please contact Carmela Dutra PO Box 610876, San Jose, CA, 95161.

Carmela Dutra
Little Katie Goes to the Moon/Carmela Dutra– [2nd] ed
p. cm.

ISBN -

1.JUVENILE NONFICTION / Science & Nature / Astronomy 2. JUVENILE NONFICTION / Science & Nature / Discoveries 3. JUVENILE NONFICTION / School & Education 4. JUVENILE NONFICTION / Adventure & Adventurers 5. JUVENILE FICTION / Science & Technology

10 9 8 7 6 5 4 3 2 1

Comments about *Little Katie Goes to the Moon* and requests for additional copies, book club rates and author speaking appearances may be addressed to Carmela Dutra PO Box 610876, San Jose, CA, 95161, or you can send your comments and requests via e-mail to carmy@carmeladutra.com or visit www.CarmelaDutra.com

Also available as an eBook from Internet retailers

Printed in the United States of America

All of the facts found in this book have been verified using the NASA website for kids, as well as Science Kids, and Cool Kid Facts.

Wouldn't it be fun to wake up one day and take a trip to the moon!? Well, that's just what little Katie did!

She loved everything about outer space, especially the moon. She knew that one day she would travel there, and today was that day!

There were a lot of things Katie learned about the moon, and she even heard people say there's a man in the moon! Little Katie wanted to see for herself if that was true.

Before Katie and her puppy, Smudge, could go to the moon, they needed to put on special space suits that would keep them warm and allow them to breathe.

AFTER GETTING DRESSED, THEY HOPPED INTO THEIR ROCKET SHIP AND STARTED COUNTING DOWN.

10   9

8

7   6

5   4

3

2

1

BLAST OFF!!

The launch was a little bumpy at first, but once they got out of the earth's atmosphere, it was smooth flying. It was so pretty in outer space! There were so many twinkling stars, and look! There's Halley's comet! Katie remembered learning about Halley's comet in school.

Do you remember learning about comets? A comet is shaped like a peanut and it has a tail. Comets are made mostly of ice and they are very old. When they get too close to the sun, some of the ice melts off and becomes gas.

As the rocket ship raced towards the moon, they passed all kinds of manmade satellites.

"Do you know why satellites are important, Smudge?" Katie asked her puppy. "Ruff?" barked Smudge, as he looked up at her.

"It's because satellites take pictures of space, and that helps scientists to learn more about our solar system!" she answered.

Finally, little Katie and Smudge made it to the moon! They had to be careful though, when landing their rocket ship, because the moon has lots of craters.

Do you know what a crater is? Craters form when big rocks hit the moon at different speeds. Unlike Earth, the moon doesn't have an atmosphere to protect it from getting hit.

They did it! They landed on the moon! Little Katie felt just like Neil Armstrong as she was stepping out of the ship.

Since there is no wind on the moon, she could still see the footprints the astronauts left behind.

WHAT DO YOU THINK IT'S LIKE TO WALK ON THE MOON? UNLIKE THE EARTH, THERE IS NO GRAVITY ON THE MOON TO HOLD YOU DOWN. SO WALKING CAN BE A LOT OF FUN! JUST BE CAREFUL NOT TO JUMP TOO HIGH, OR YOU MIGHT NOT COME BACK DOWN.

LITTLE KATIE AND SMUDGE LEAPED AND SKIPPED ACROSS THE MOON, DISCOVERING MANY THINGS! FIRST, THEY SAW THE LUNAR LASER RANGING EXPERIMENT. DO YOU KNOW WHAT THIS IS? WHO DO YOU THINK LEFT IT BEHIND?

YOU GUESSED IT! BUZZ ALDRIN AND NEIL ARMSTRONG PUT IT ON THE MOON BEFORE THEY LEFT TO COME BACK HOME, AND LOOK— IT'S STILL HERE, WORKING TOO!

THIS IS A SPECIAL MACHINE THAT MEASURES THE DISTANCE BETWEEN THE EARTH AND THE MOON USING RETRO-REFLECTING MIRRORS.

"RUFF- RUFF!!!"

LITTLE KATIE GRINNED AND SAID, "I AGREE, SMUDGE, LET'S KEEP GOING AND SEE WHAT ELSE WE CAN FIND!"
AS THEY BUNNY-HOPPED ACROSS THE MOON, THEY FOUND THE SPECIALLY-MADE FLAG THAT THE ASTRONAUTS LEFT.

"BAAARRROOO!" CRIED SMUDGE AS HE PATTED THE GROUND. "YOU'RE RIGHT, SMUDGE! THIS IS JUST LIKE WHAT NEIL ARMSTRONG SAID: 'THAT'S ONE SMALL STEP FOR MAN, ONE GIANT LEAP FOR MANKIND.'"

SMUDGE, LOOK!" KATIE EXCITEDLY SHOUTED, POINTING AT THE BEAUTIFUL BLUE PLANET. "THAT'S OUR HOME!" "ARF- ARF!!!" "NO, SMUDGE, WE CAN'T JUMP HOME. IT'S TOO FAR."

CAN YOU GUESS HOW FAR AWAY EARTH IS FROM THE MOON? THE MOON TRAVELS AROUND THE EARTH IN AN ELLIPTICAL ORBIT. THE DISTANCE VARIES, BUT IT'S STILL OVER 230,000 MILES AWAY!

Even when the moon is at its closest, it is 223,700 miles away from the earth. So if you were riding in a car going 70 miles per hour, it would take you 135 days to get there!

Imagine how long it would take when the moon is at its farthest away from the earth!

ALL OF A SUDDEN, SMUDGE TOOK OFF, JUMPING BACK TOWARDS THE ROCKET SHIP. LITTLE KATIE QUICKLY BUNNY-HOPPED AFTER HIM.

"WHY DID YOU LEAP AWAY SMUDGE?" SHE ASKED. THEN THERE WAS A SMALL RUMBLE. "DID YOU FEEL THAT??" "GRRRUFFF!" "I THINK THAT WAS A SMALL QUAKE!"

DID YOU KNOW THAT THE MOON HAS SMALL QUAKES? WELL IT DOES! THEY ARE SMALL MOONQUAKES, SEVERAL MILES BELOW THE SURFACE. THEY ARE THOUGHT TO BE CAUSED BY THE GRAVITATIONAL PULL OF THE EARTH.

LITTLE KATIE AND SMUDGE DECIDED IT WAS TIME TO GO HOME, SO THEY CLIMBED INSIDE THE ROCKET SHIP AND BLASTED OFF.

"WOOF-WOOF?" SMUDGE YAPPED. "OH, I DID HAVE FUN, SMUDGE," LITTLE KATIE WHISPERED, "I JUST WISHED I COULD'VE FOUND OUT IF THE STORIES ABOUT THE MAN IN THE MOON WERE TRUE."

THEN, AS SHE LOOKED OUT THE WINDOW, SHE SAW HIM! ONLY, IT WASN'T REALLY A MAN. THE MOON HAS DARK SPOTS, OR PATCHES, AND SOME PEOPLE SAY THE DARK SPOTS LOOK LIKE EYES AND A SMILE. SO THAT'S WHY SOME PEOPLE SAY THERE IS A MAN IN THE MOON!

"It's time to stop playing now sweetie, lunch is ready!" Little Katie looked up and saw Momma standing there, smiling at her. "Did you have fun playing in the rocket ship you built?"

"Oh yes! Smudge and i Bunny hopped across the moon, we felt a moonquake, and even saw the man in the moon!" "Wow! That sounds like a lot of fun!" responded Momma.

"Maybe someday, you can go to the moon for real!" Little Katie whispered to herself, "One day i will!"

Glossary

Astronauts: A person who is trained to travel in a spacecraft.

Atmosphere: The gaseous area surrounding a planet or other body.

Buzz Aldrin: He and flight commander Neil Armstrong made the Apollo 11 moonwalk in 1969.He was one of the first two humans to land on the Moon, and the second person to walk on it.

Comet: Comets are made of ice, dust and small rocky particles.

Crater: A large, bowl-shaped cavity in the ground or on the surface of a planet or the moon.

Elliptical Orbit: A small body in space orbits a larger one along an elliptical path.

Gravity: The force which tries to pull two objects toward each other.

Halley's Comet: Halley's Comet (or Comet Halley as it is also known) is the most well-known comet.

Moonquakes: Moonquakes are quakes that occur on the moon similar to earthquakes, but are weaker than earthquakes.

Neil Armstrong: An American astronaut and the first person to walk on the Moon.

Retro-Reflecting Mirrors: A device or surface that reflects light back to its source.

Rocket Ship: A vehicle that uses an engine to launch into space.

Satellite: An artificial object that is deliberately sent into orbit in space, usually in order to send, receive or bounce back information to different areas of Earth.

Spacesuit: A spacesuit provides protection and a means for survival for the astronaut.